THIS BOOK IS DEDICATED TO MY WONDERFUL WIFE, LUCY, WHOSE BRILLIANT IDEA IT WAS, AND WHO'S BEEN WAITING, SOMEWHAT PATIENTLY, FOR OVER TWENTY YEARS FOR ME TO DO A CHILDREN'S BOOK! I HOPE THIS IS JUST THE FIRST OF MANY. I'D ALSO LIKE TO THANK MY WHOLE FAMILY FOR THEIR CONSTANT LOVING SUPPORT AND HELP, AND ALSO THE EMMAUS PUBLIC LIBRARY STAFF FOR THEIR ENTHUSIASTIC ENCOURAGEMENT. SPECIAL THANKS TO LISA DUGAN FOR HER INVALUABLE ASSISTANCE CONNECTING ME WITH HARPERCOLLINS, AND TO MARGARET, MY SUPEREDITOR.

To BRITAIN!! 06

Bob McLeod

SuperHero ABC
Copyright © 2006 by Bob McLeod
Manufactured in China.

Library of Congress Cataloging-in-Publication Data
McLeod, Bob. SuperHero ABC / by Bob McLeod. — 1st ed. p. cm. Summary: Humorous SuperHeroes such as Goo Girl and The Volcano represent the letters of the alphabet from A to Z. ISBN-10: 0-06-074514-2 — ISBN-10: 0-06-074515-0 (lib. bdg.) ISBN-13: 978-0-06-074514-1 — ISBN-13: 978-0-06-074515-8 (lib. bdg.)
[1. Heroes—Fiction. 2. Alphabet.] I. Title. PZ7.M478716Su 2006 2004022180 [E]—dc22 CIP AC

Typography by Meredith Pratt
12 13 14 15 16 SCP 20 19 18 17 16 15 14 13 12 11
❖
First Edition

SUPERHERO ABC

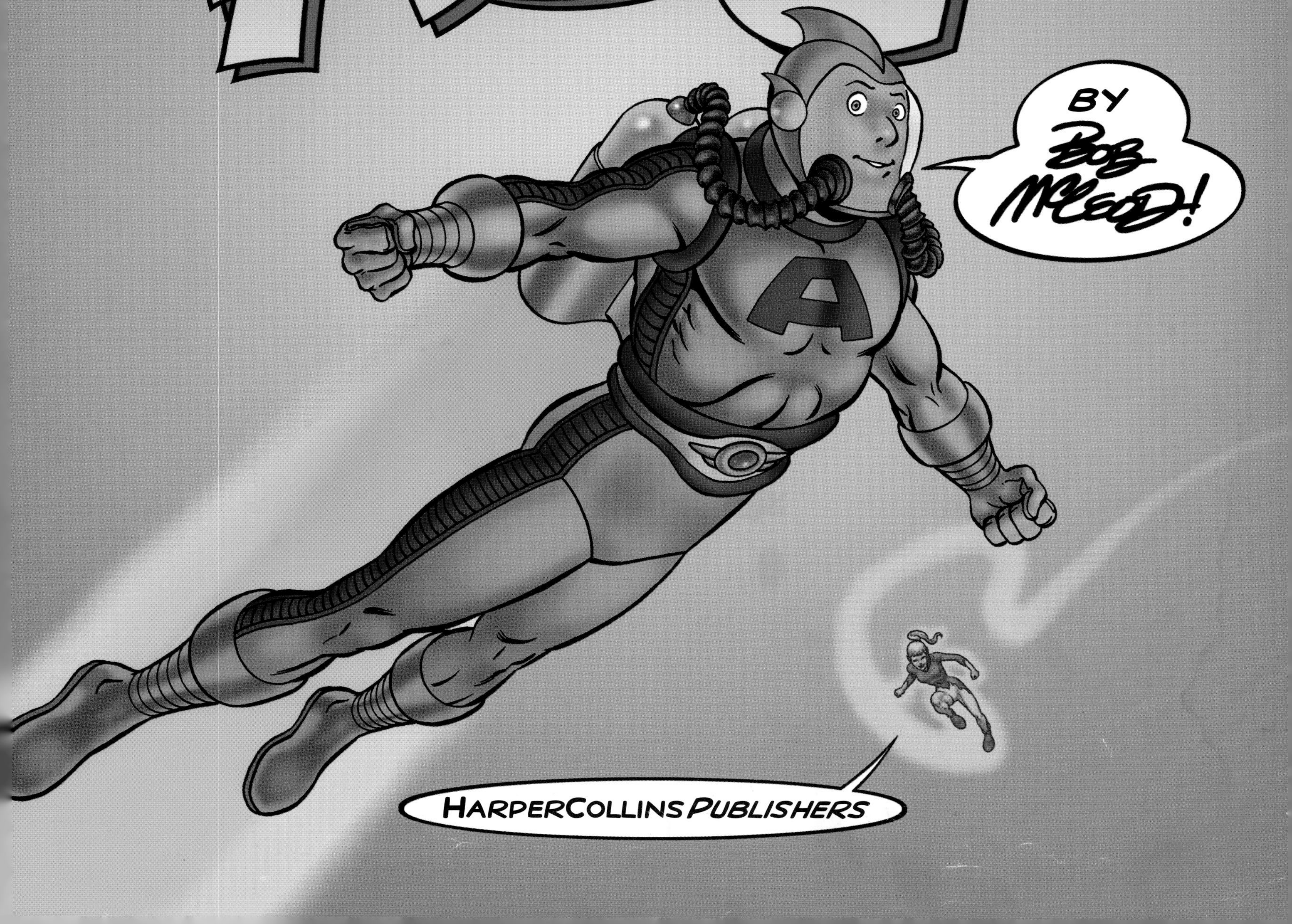

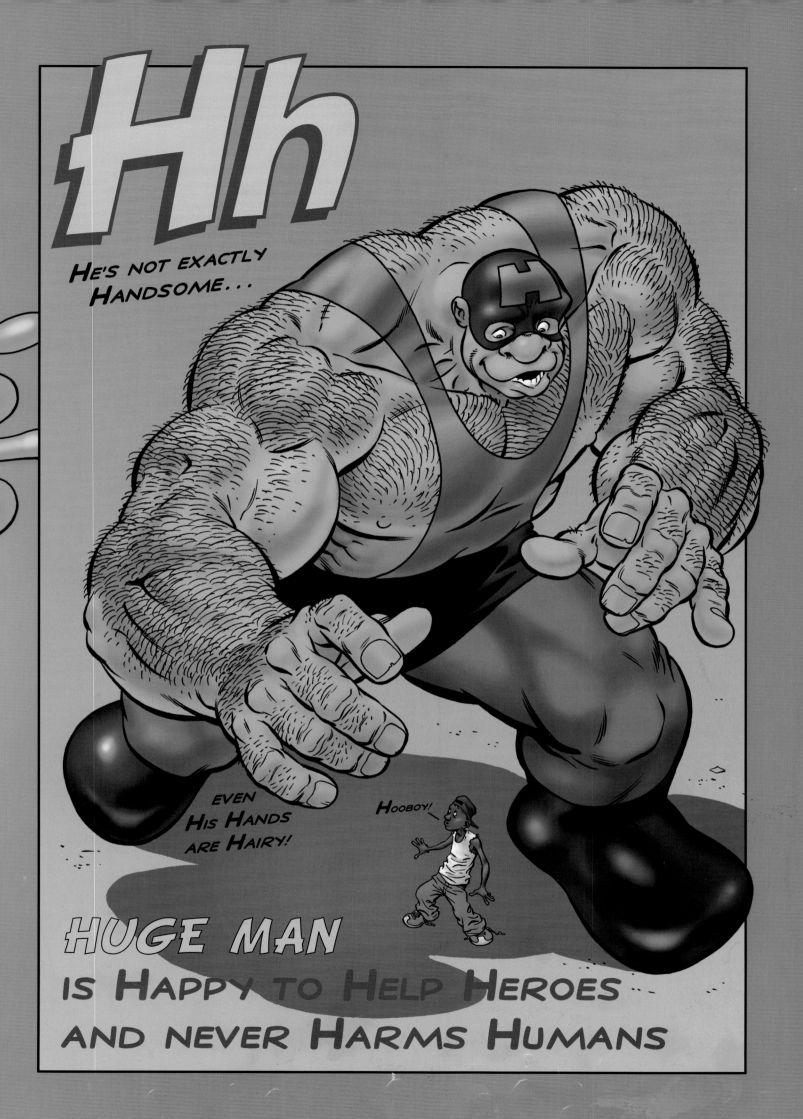

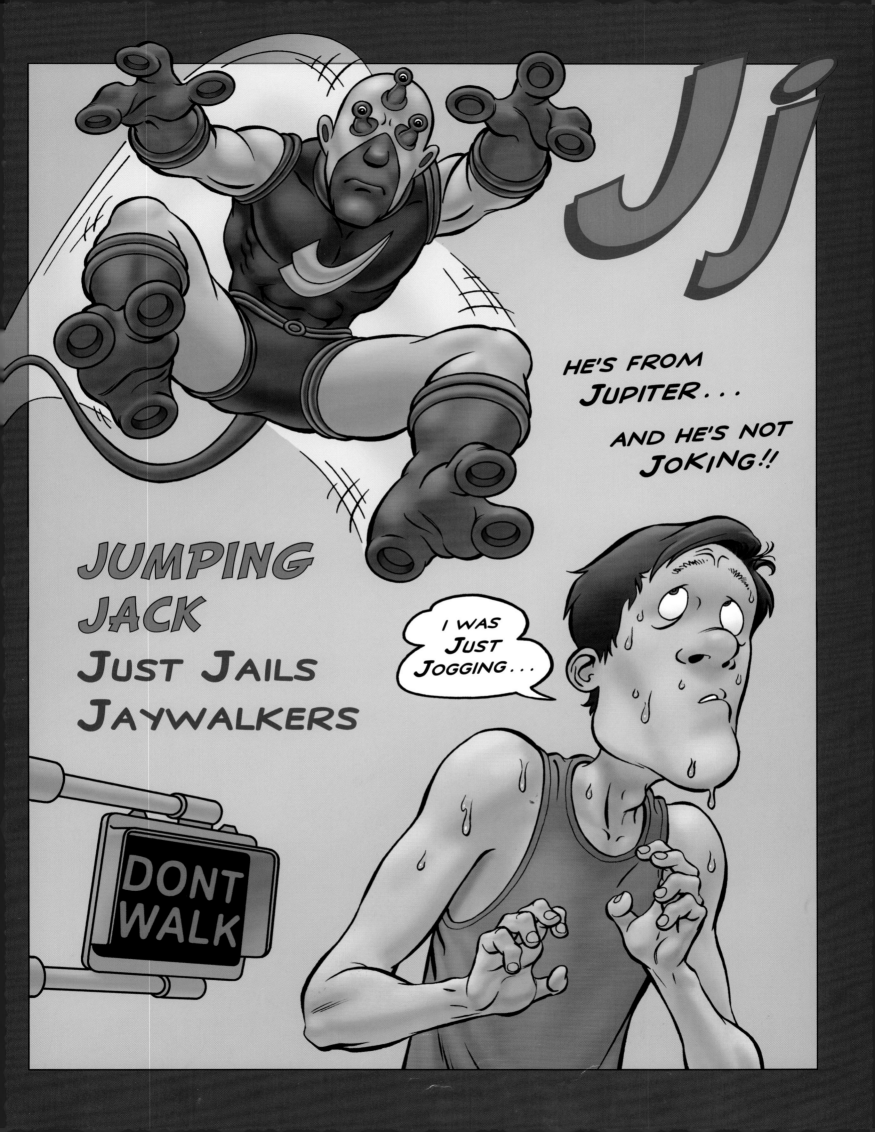

Mm

HE WEARS A MASK!

MULTIPLYING MIKE BECOMES MANY MORE MEN IN MOMENTS

HE HAS MIGHTY MUSCLES!

HIS MOM MAKES THEM ALL MIND THEIR MANNERS!

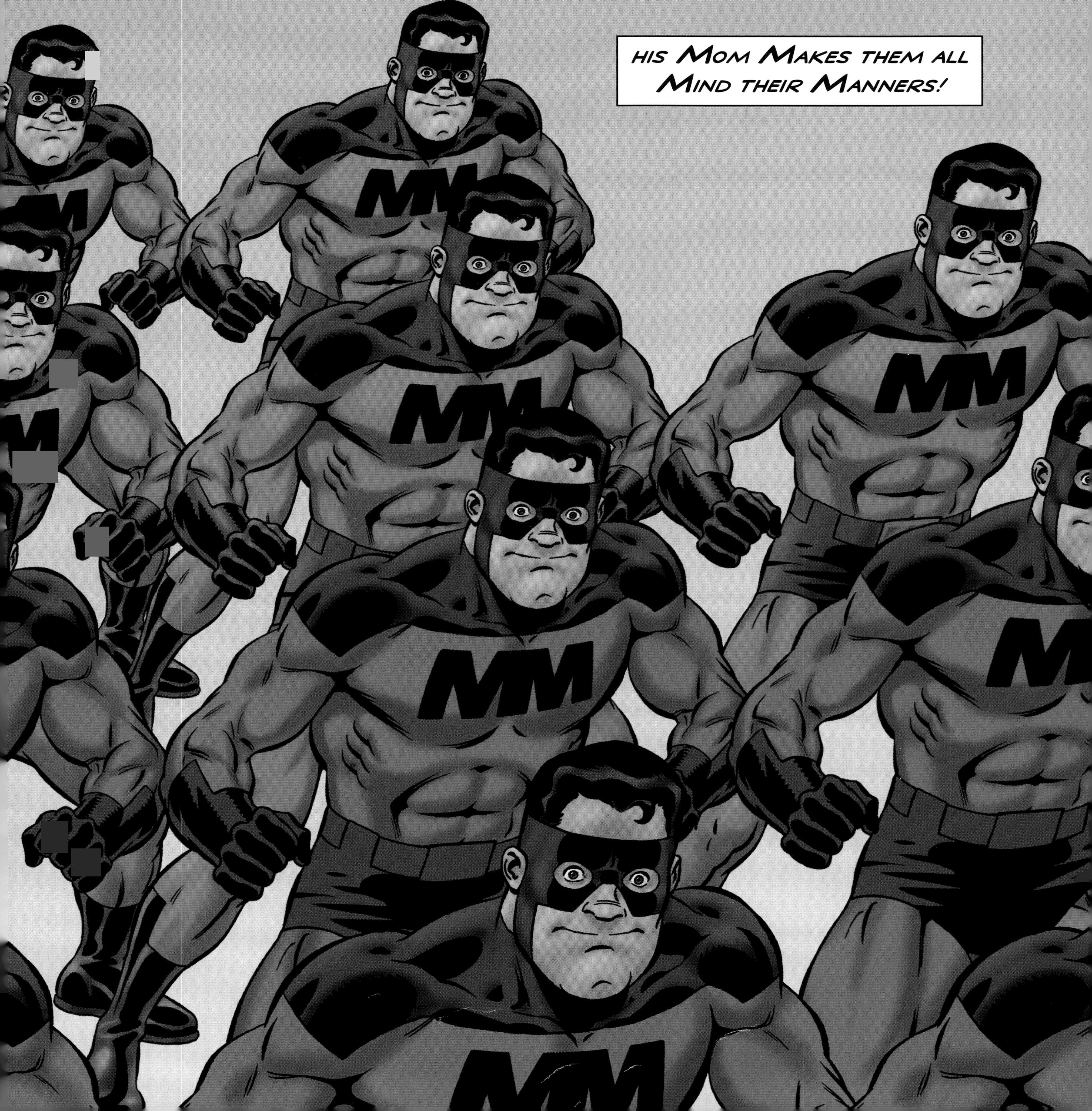

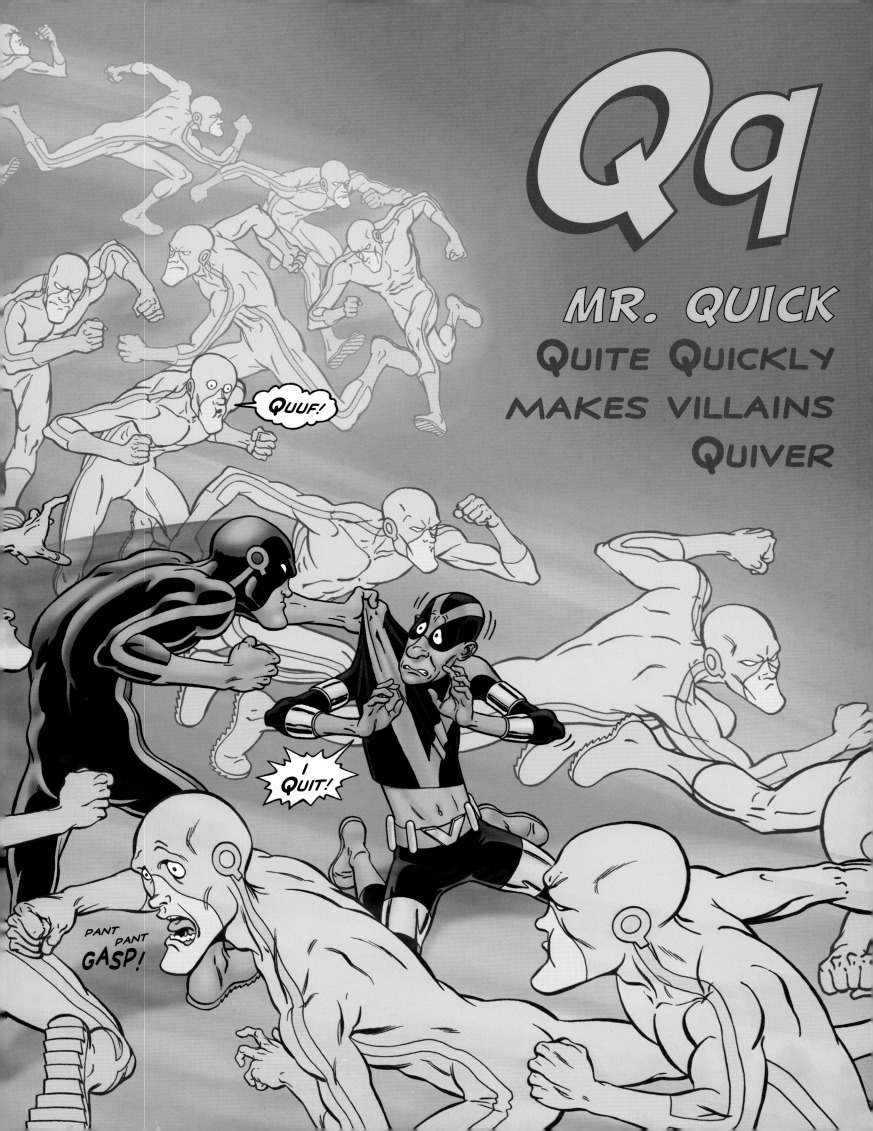

Rr

HIS COSTUME
IS RED
RUBBER!
REALLY!

RATS!

HE'S A RIOT!

BUT RATHER RUDE...

SKY-BOY
SOARS THROUGH THE SKY AFTER SCHOOL
Ss
HE'S ONLY SEVEN!
AND SO DOES HIS SISTER!
SHE'S SIX!

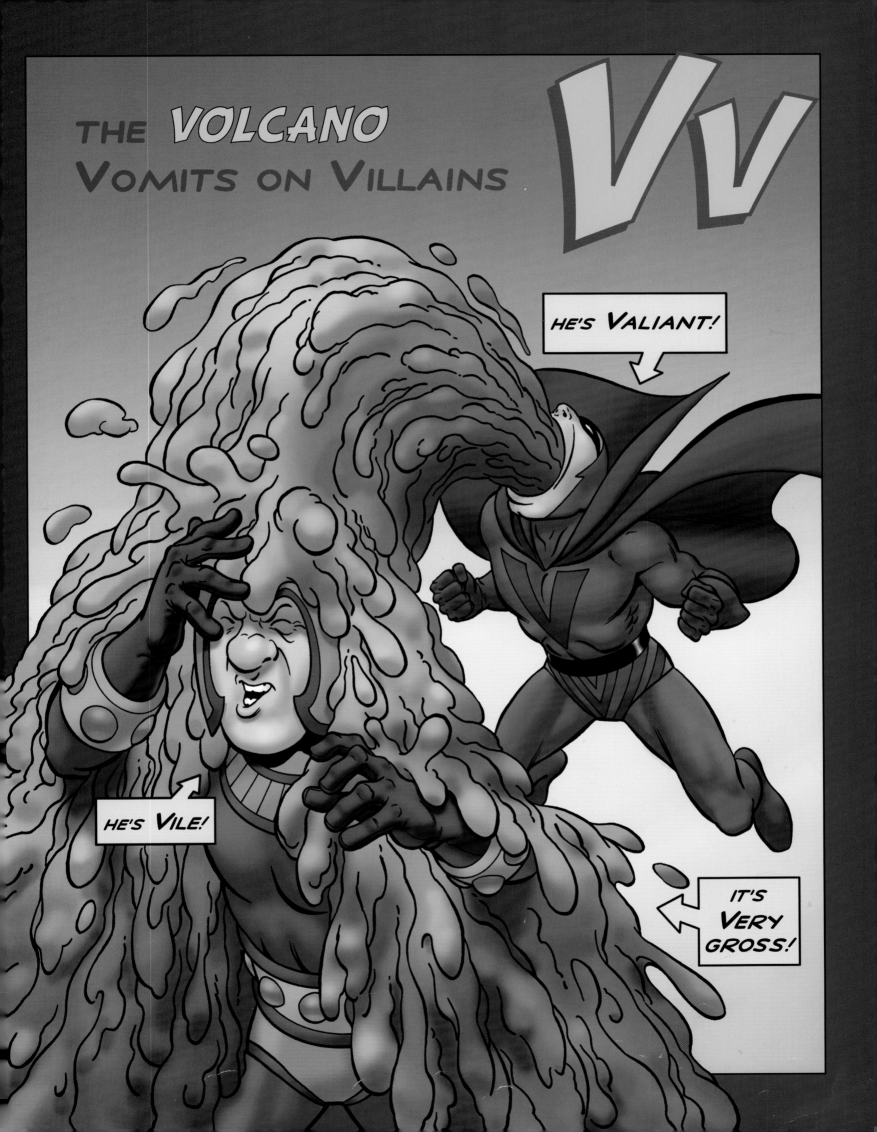

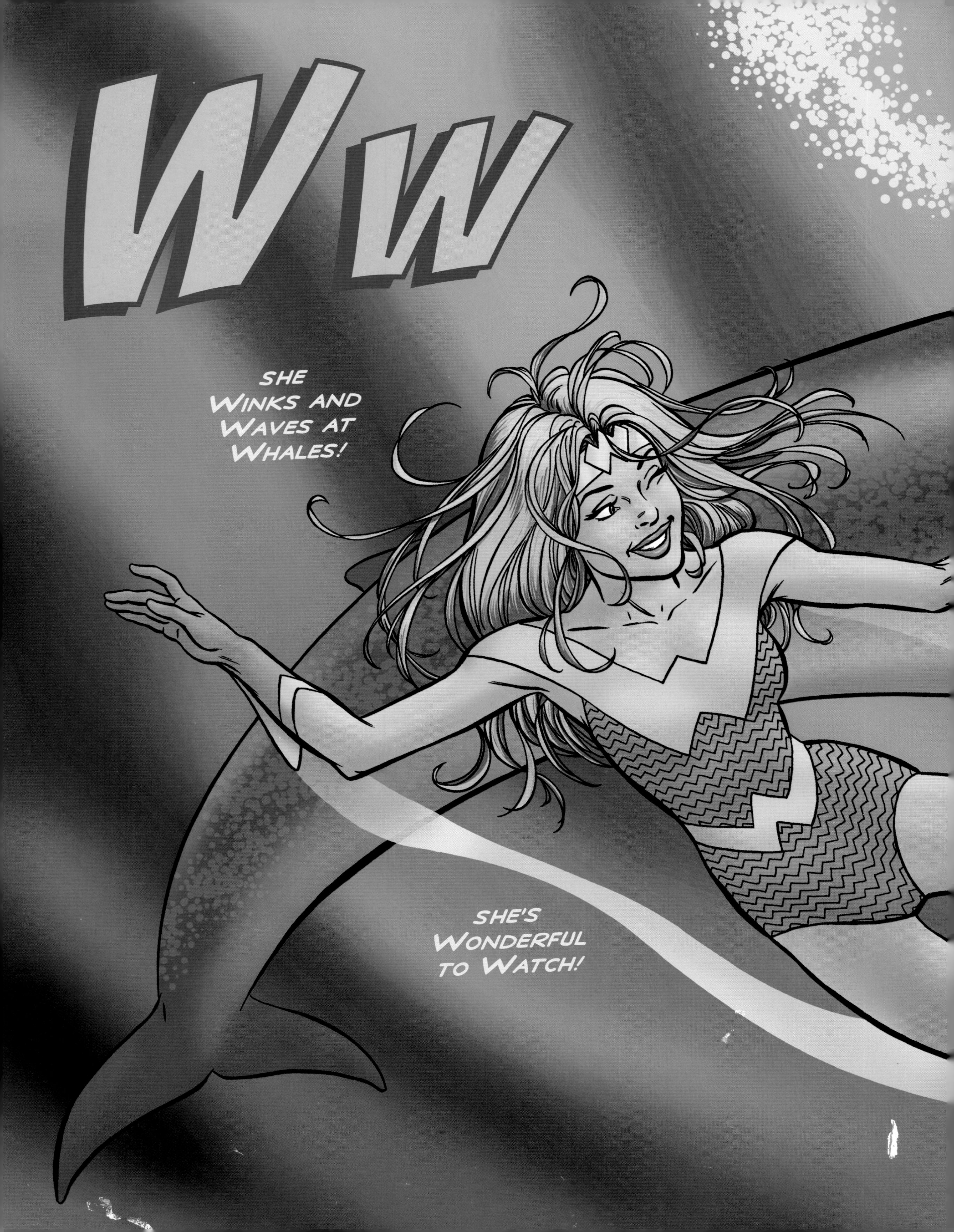
Ww
She Winks and Waves at Whales!
She's Wonderful to Watch!

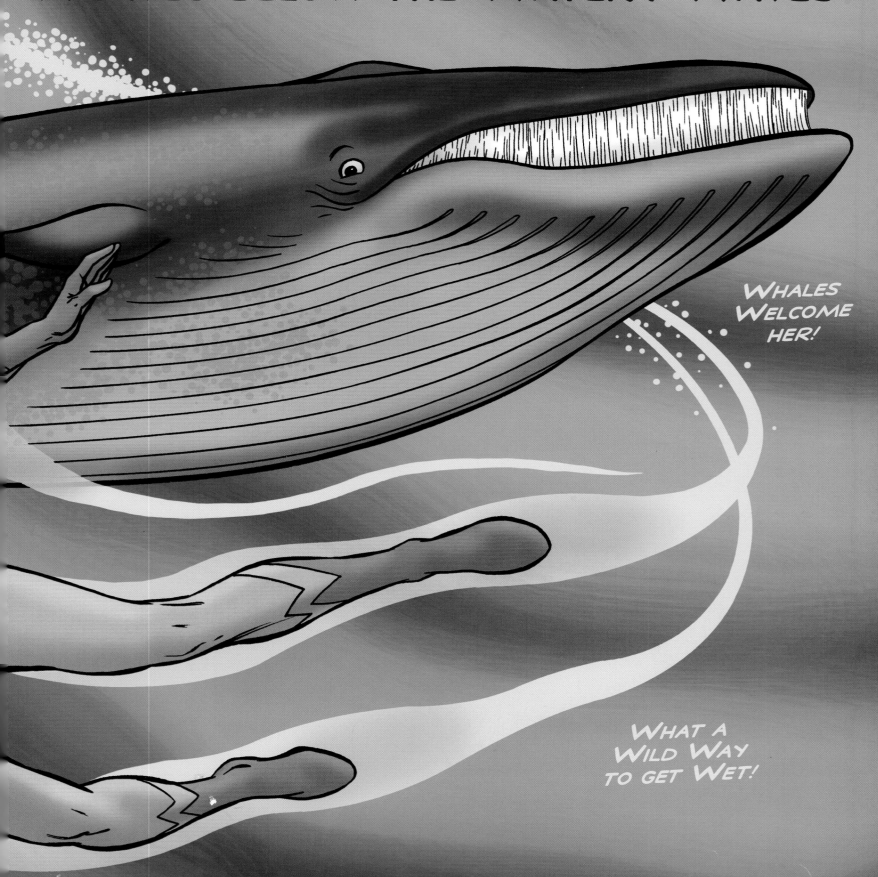

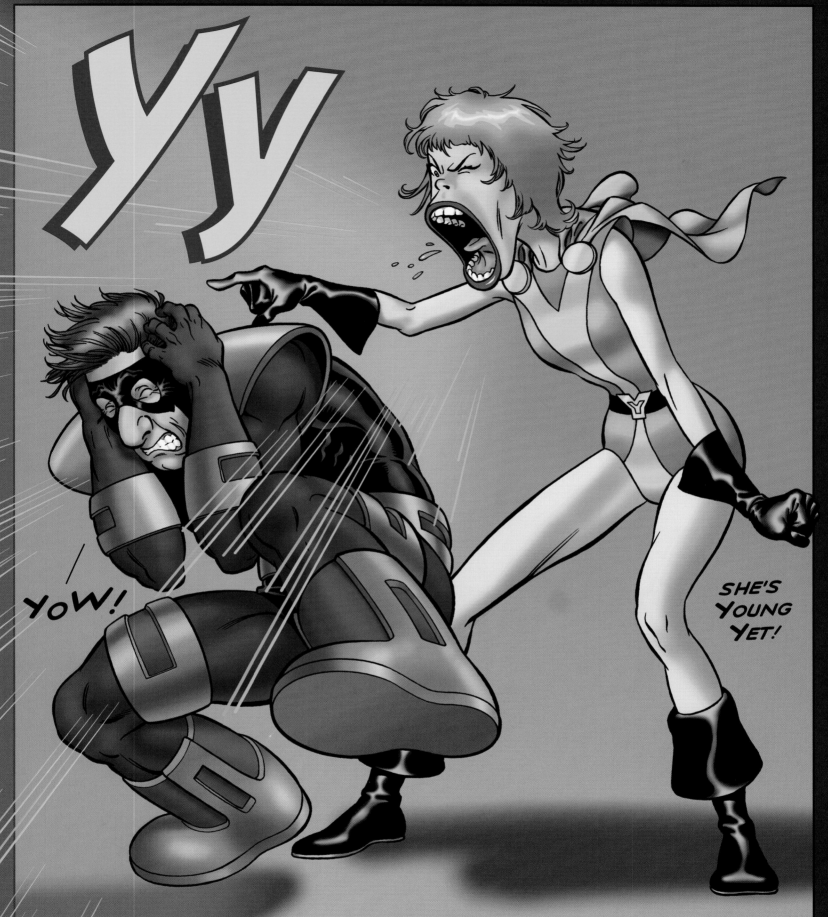

The **ZINGER**
Zanily Zigzags through
the Zero Zone